Come On Over to Barney's House!

Written by Stephen White
Illustrated by Darren McKee

Ding-dong! Ding-dong!
The doorbell was ringing
at Barney's house.

"Hi, Barney!" said Claire.
"Robert and I came
over to play with you."

"We want to play with
Baby Bop and BJ, too!"
added Robert.

"Super-dee-duper!"
chuckled Barney, as
he opened the door.
"You're always welcome
at my house!"

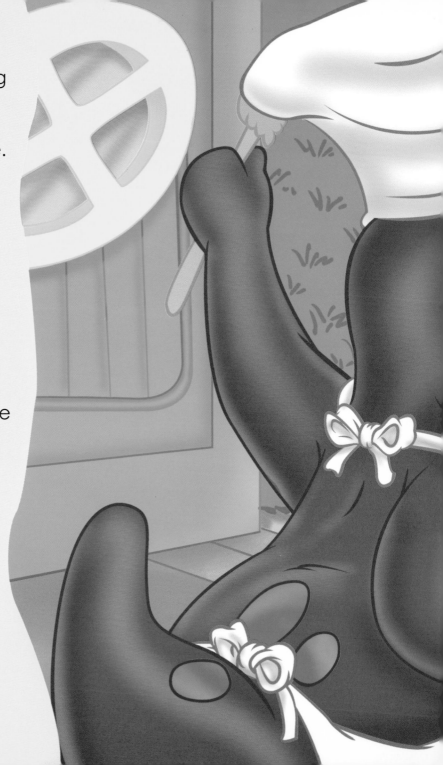

"I was just making peanut butter and jelly sandwiches with my handy-dandy PB&J Machine," said Barney. "Would you like to see how it works?"

"We sure would!" answered Claire and Robert.

Barney showed them how to pour peanuts in the PB&J Machine to make peanut butter. Then they added grapes to make the jelly.

"Mmmmm," said Robert, as he gobbled up the gooey sandwich. "De-yum-licious!"

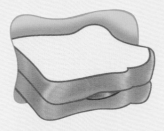

Just then, Claire spotted
Baby Bop across the room!

"Hi, Baby Bop!" exclaimed
Claire, hugging her friend.
"What are you playing with?"

"This is Barney's Spin-the-
Globe Radio," giggled
Baby Bop. "It plays pretty
music from around the world!"

Barney showed Robert
and Claire how the radio
worked. "Spin the globe,"
said Barney, "and you'll
hear music from the country
where the pointer stops!"

"Watch this!" said Baby Bop, wildly spinning the globe.

"Wow! I hear salsa music from Mexico!" exclaimed Robert.

"And now I hear a happy jig from Scotland!" added Barney.

"BJ and I love listening to all kinds of music!" added Baby Bop, as the globe stopped spinning and the music faded away.

Robert looked around.
"By the way, where is BJ?" he wondered.

"I think BJ was playing on the computer earlier," said Barney.

BJ wasn't at the computer,
but someone else was!

"Robert and Claire, I'd like
you to meet my friend Murray,
the Web-surfing mouse,"
said Barney.

"Wow!" cried Claire. "I've
never seen a computer
mouse like you before!"

"Murray, do you know where
BJ is?" asked Robert.

"I can find all kinds of cool
things on my computer, dude,
but it won't tell me where BJ is,"
replied Murray. "Why don't we
look upstairs?"

Everyone crowded into the Upsy-Daisy elevator.

"May I please push the button to make us go up?" asked Baby Bop.

"Yes, you may!" laughed Barney. "Up we go!"

"Upsy-daisy!" exclaimed Murray.

Upstairs, Claire and Robert stepped into a long hallway lined with fun-looking doors.

"There are lots of rooms up here," said Barney, "and each one has a different surprise!"

"Let's see what's behind door number three!" laughed Murray.

Baby Bop and Claire entered a room filled with pippity-popping bubbles! *Pop! Pop! Pop!*

"These bubbles tickle!" Baby Bop giggled, as a bubble popped on her nose.

"They sure do!" laughed Claire. "But I don't see BJ in here!"

Barney, Robert and Murray entered a room filled with a bazillion bouncing balls! *Boing! Boing! Boing! Boing!*

"I feel like bouncing, too!" Barney chuckled, as he hopped up and down.

"So do I!" laughed Murray. "But I don't see BJ in here!"

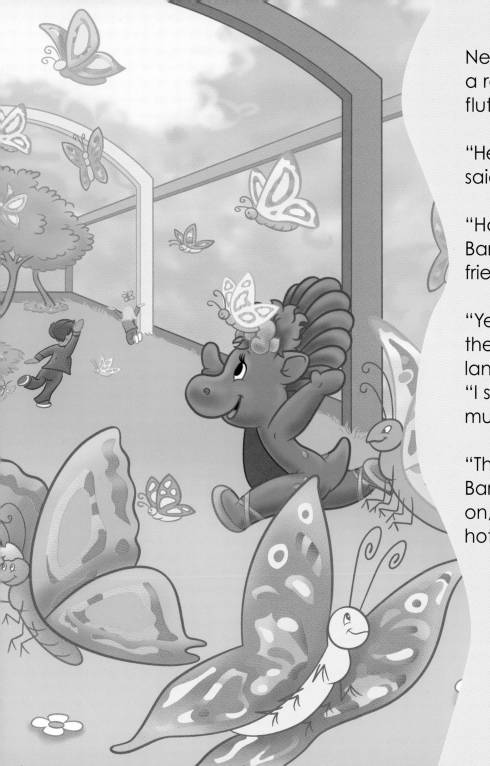

Next, they looked into a room filled with fluttering butterflies!

"Hello, pretty butterflies!" said Baby Bop.

"Have you seen BJ?" Barney asked a friendly butterfly.

"Yes," answered Betty the Butterfly, as she landed on his hand. "I saw BJ in the music room."

"Thank you!" said Barney. "Come on, everyone! We're hot on the trail of BJ!"

In the music room, Murray found a piano that went *plink-plink-plunk*, and Barney found a drum that went *ratta-tatta-tat*! But they didn't find BJ!

"Where, oh, where could BJ be?" cried Baby Bop.

"Chill, everybody," cawed the super-cool Mr. Bluejay from the window. "Listen up, and I'll tell you where BJ is!"

Mr. Bluejay rocked from side to side as he sang.

*"BJ was just up here
Gettin' things for his surprise,
And now he's waitin' downstairs,
For all you gals and guys!"*

Barney and his friends hurried downstairs, and sure enough, there was BJ! He was setting up drums and keyboards with John and Evelyn, two friends from the neighborhood.

"Hi, guys!" said BJ. "Are you ready for my big surprise? We've started a rock 'n' roll band – and we want to play for you!"

"That sounds super-dee-duper!" laughed Barney.

BJ and the Rockets rocked
out while everyone
danced along!

"Go, BJ, go!" laughed Murray.

Suddenly, balloons and
confetti rained down
from the ceiling, as
Barney danced over to
the center of the room.

"Watch this!" cried Barney.
"It's called the Dino Dance!"

"First you hop, hop, hop
All over the place!
Shake your dino tail
While you make a funny face!
Everybody start twisting and turning,
We'll have a lot of fun while we're learning
To do the Dino Dance!"

"I'm so glad we came to visit you today, Barney!" said Claire. "Your house is full of surprises – just like you!"

"I hope you come back soon!" chuckled their big purple friend. "It's always playtime at Barney's house!"